Saving Private Woods

First published 2012 by Fast-Print Publishing of
Peterborough, England.

www.fast-print.net/store.php

Saving Private Woods
Copyright © Shelly Kaye 2012

ISBN: 978-178035-510-8

All characters are fictional.
Any similarity to any actual person is purely coincidental.

A catalogue record for this book is available from the British Library

An environmentally friendly book printed and bound in England by
www.printondemand-worldwide.com

Mixed Sources
Product group from well-managed
forests, and other controlled sources
www.fsc.org Cert no. TT-COC-002641
© 1996 Forest Stewardship Council
FSC

PEFC Certified
This product is
from sustainably
managed forests
and controlled
sources
PEFC
PEFC/16-33-415
www.pefc.org

This book is made entirely of chain-of-custody materials

The Author

Shelly Kaye has worked in childcare for over 25 years.

Whilst at school she was a regular babysitter for neighbours. Then, after qualifying at college, she became a nanny to several families before moving on to manage nurseries and crèches.

One of four children, she spent much of her school holidays playing freely in Hatfield Park, with her siblings, cousins and friends, and so came to love the area and its incredible history.

She always kindled an interest in wildlife, art, poetry and writing, and was persuaded to pen a series of children's stories. These are infused with some of her own 1960s childhood capers and complemented by her career long experiences as a storyteller to countless children.

Special thanks to:
Aidan Hickey
Without whose guidance, these stories would not have
been written.

Illustrated by Ric Machin

Colourist: Katy Lloyd

INTRODUCTION

In the beginning... there were Hobtails - small, kind, folk with fantastic memories - who can live to be 500 years old.

Their cosy Hobhouse home is down in the disused chalk mine tunnels that run everywhere under the ancient town of Hatfield.

Legend has it, that the Hobtails were born to look after wild animals and birds, the rivers and trees.

But when humans suddenly arrived on the scene, many hundreds of years ago, they found themselves with far more to deal with than ever before!

Hobtails usually try to avoid contact with people, but they're often busy, secretly sorting out man made problems with their heron friend, Wing Commander Pellington.

And epic adventures abound over the smallest things!

THE HOBTAILS

GASCOYNE

MORTIMERRY

NAN DAISY

COCO LEGUME

TALBOT

ONSLOW

DUNC

FLOSSIE JO

PELLINGTON

CONTENTS

Chapter 1
MILITARY MATTERS

With hardly a flap of his broad wings, Pellington circled gracefully, high above the abandoned airfield.

He liked to imagine that it was still a busy place and that he still had the important job of shooing away the birds and rabbits from the runway when aircraft were coming in to land or about to take off. And today was like any other as he went about his daily business of checking on ground conditions. He totally ignored the fact that planes never came there anymore.

He swooped down and made a slightly dodgy landing on the roof of the control tower, which sat on top of the enormous old hangar building. With thin gangly legs, he didn't always land as neatly as smaller birds do.

He composed himself and stretched out his long neck to study the horizon over to the east; then to the north, west and south. Satisfied that all the great landmarks were exactly where they ought to be, he settled down more comfortably on the broken roof to preen some flight feathers.

Pellington is a heron. But, as can be seen from his airforce jacket, his leather cap and goggles, in his heart of hearts he's an airman. But no ordinary one. He held the rank of Wing Commander; a title, some thought, that he had awarded to himself. But nobody was quite sure, and it would be rude to ask.

Pellington had never forgotten that the skies above

Hatfield were once filled with all sorts of aircraft such as bi-planes, fighters and passenger jets. And with admiration, he had watched them develop over the years. In his personal opinion, planes weren't quite as airworthy as birds but, nonetheless, he felt that he had played a small part in those great human achievements.

And keeping creatures off the runway was certainly not a job to be sniffed at!

"Ah yes," he sighed dreamily to himself, "those were amazing times."

Then, something far below caught Pellington's beady eye. He peered down and focused hard.

Out beyond the cracked concrete of the runway – and its fine display of weeds – something made the security wire fence tremble. A small hand pushed against the mesh, revealing a gap. Moments later a head came through the opening. Pellington shuffled sideways and leant forward, staring intently at the movement.

"Mmm, that's young Mortimerry," he muttered to a pigeon perched nearby. "I wonder what mischief that young Hobtail is up to!" The pigeon ignored him.

When Mortimerry was sure there were no dangers lurking on the airfield, he climbed through a hole in the fence and stood to have another look around. "It's okay," he called. "Come on!"

Then three more Hobtails came through the hole.

At about the height of a washing machine, Mortimerry is tall for a Hobtail of his age. He is also very smart. In human terms he would be about ten years old, but Hobtails age very slowly.

The ones who came through the fence after Mortimerry were Coco Legume, Flossie Jo and Onslow. Coco came through extra carefully, worried about tearing her pretty pink dress. But Flossie Jo moved quicker because she wore tough denim dungarees. But quickest of all was Onslow, because being so small he could squirm through easily.

Now, in case you're wondering, Hobtails are kindly creatures who have lived in these parts for a very, very long time. They were here even before people arrived. Day after day they roam all over the countryside and the town but they are very good at keeping out of sight. As a matter of fact, if you're over ten yourself you may never have the ability to see them. And to make matters more mysterious, they spend half their time in their cosy little home called the Hobhouse, down in the old chalk mine tunnels beneath the fields and streets of Hatfield.

3

On this day, all of them were carrying tin cans with wire handles. Seeing Hobtails with cans like this means only one thing: they're off to gather fruit.

Big Dunc was the last one to arrive at the fence. The hole was a good fit for his head but the rest of him got stuck. He struggled and shoved so hard that the wire mesh stretched. But all he managed to do was to tear his collar.

"Oh!" said Dunc, surprised and annoyed. "Why can't I get through? You lot got through. It's not fair!"

"You're stuck because you eat too much!" snapped Flossie Jo, without even looking at him.

"She means you're just a bit too big, mon cherie!" laughed Coco.

Now, Hobtails may indeed be very kind-hearted, good to animals and that sort of thing – but they're not always patient with one another.

"Stop moaning!" Mortimerry said. "Just go and find a bigger gap for yourself!"

The fence shook and twanged as Dunc pulled his

4

head out of the wire. This caused his baseball cap to fall off and flop down, out of reach, on the wrong side of the fence. It lay on the grass by Mortimerry's feet.

"Pass my cap, will you?" said Dunc.

"What, this one? Your favourite?" Mort teased. Then he placed it on young Onslow's head and ushered him away. Coco and Flossie walked off too.

"Oi, give it me back!" yelled Dunc in helpless frustration.

Mortimery replied, "Well, you'd better hurry up and join us, Dunc. You know what Onslow's like for losing things!"

Dunc was now very cross and he raced along the fence, searching for a hole big enough to get through, moaning as he went, "I'm not too big. I'm just well developed, that's all! Huh!"

Mortimerry looked over towards the hangar and up to the control tower. "Hey, there's Pellington!" he said, pointing him out. "Hello, Wing Commander."

The heron gave them a slow and careful salute. The Hobtails waved back.

Coco stared at him with admiration. The heron still cut a dashing figure in the uniform that she had made for him all those years ago. And she wondered if the addition of a little more gold braid on his jacket would be appropriate.....or, perhaps, a medal.

"Why is Pellington always hanging around here?" asked Onslow.

"Oh, he still likes to think about the aircraft and the war," said Mortimerry.

5

Dunc's voice suddenly boomed out behind them. "What war?" he said, and snatched back his cap from Onslow's head.

The others jumped. They hadn't heard him come rushing up. "The World War!" said Flossie Jo. She frowned at Dunc, then led the gang into the huge, but deserted aircraft hangar, where parts of old planes were still lying around among broken glass, and rusting equipment lay in puddles. "Back then bombs crashed down around here. Don't you remember?"

Coco shuddered. "I do. It was awful."

"Awful messy, I bet, " said Dunc, whose memory usually only stretched back as far as his last dinner.

The Hobtails stood in silence, thinking of those long-gone days - all except Dunc, of course, who was now checking his baseball cap for damage.

They decided to leave the old hangar and made their way back across the runway towards the woods. Soon, they came upon an untidy pile of broken-up aeroplanes which had been made out of canvas cloth and metal tube frames. Dunc pointed to them and asked, "Are those from the war time?"

"No," said Mortimerry. "I think the film-makers left those behind a few years ago. We came here once. Don't you remember? Apparently it was a really famous war film." Dunc shook his head.

"I remember it well," said Flossie Jo. "It was called *Saving Private Ryan.* The story was about a lost soldier, and I'm sure they made the film here much more noisy than a real war."

"And it nearly made me cry," said Coco, "'cos I thought they'd blown up the pretty old gamekeeper's cottage in the woods. But they were only pretending." Flossie Jo nodded. "They pretend about everything in films. It's all make-believe."

Coco laughed."Yes, that's what I like about the cinema. You can make anything seem real!"

The five Hobtails walked past weather-beaten props left by the film-makers: broken wooden guns, a searchlight, rotting boots, rope nets and a sign that said: 'Danger! Unexploded Mines'

Mortimerry stooped to pick up a soldier's helmet. He tipped out some rain water, gave it a wipe, and put it on his head. It was far too big and sank down over his eyes, but he marched about like a soldier saying, "Private Ryan on parade:Left, right. Left, right. Left..."

Of course he couldn't see, and he marched into Dunc's back, jerking him forward. Dunc thought he was being attacked. He swung round and gave Mort a karate chop on the helmet, knocking it down further over his face. Mort fell to the ground, and his muffled voice moaned. "Hey! What d'you think you're doing?"

When Mort finally took off the helmet, Dunc was quite surprised to see who was wearing it.

"Oh, it's *you*, Mort" he said. "Sorry. I thought it was that Private Ryan soldier, trying to pinch my baseball cap."

Mort rubbed his head. "Why would I or anybody else, want your silly cap? It wouldn't fit anyway!" he replied. "Come on, everybody! Let's go before Dunc imagines he's being attacked again!"

Soon after this, the gang ambled off and entered some

woodland called Home Covert. In a clearing among the trees, they came across a row of three brick-built sheds, like garages, and each had a heavy steel door.

"I remember these," said Mort. "When the fighter planes were made in Hatfield, they used to test their guns up here, and they kept the dangerous stuff locked up in those sheds."

"What sort of stuff?" Flossie Jo asked.

Mortimerry shrugged. "Er, bullets and bombs, I guess. Things that flash, go 'bang!' and cause a fire."

"You mean 'inflammable' things," said Coco, quite proud of her knowledge. She was also quite excited to be on the site where a famous film was made, because she loved the idea of being an actress in a movie.

The young Hobtails walked over to have a look. The door on the first shed was partly open, so they peeped inside. As they did so, a small bird flew out, making them all jump.

"A robin! Yeah, that's really dangerous!" said Dunc. Mortimerry glared at him. The place was empty... and it didn't smell very nice. They went to the next shed, but there was nothing much in it either, apart from a mouldy sleeping bag on the floor, some ashes from a fire, a saucepan and a coffee jar with just a bit of coffee left in it.

Clearly, somebody had stayed in there at one time, and Dunc took more interest in this than anyone else. Turning from the shed, he saw a big sign nailed to a tree, and read it out to the others. "Look, it says here: 'PRIVATE... WOODS... KEEP... OUT!'"

He thought about this for a moment, then said, "Obviously there's only one place they'd want to keep him out of... "

The other Hobtails looked at him quizzically.

"Keep who, out of where?" asked Flossie Jo.

"Private Woods, of course," replied Dunc. "And the only place they'd want to keep him out of is that shed with the sleeping bag in it."

Mort, Onslow, Flossie Jo and Coco looked at one another in confusion. And Dunc looked back at them the same way. He found it hard to believe that they couldn't understand what the sign meant. So he tried again. "Look, it's simple. Private Woods must've been working on that film with Private Ryan. But he kept sneaking off to sleep in that shed, and to drink coffee. So they put up that warning sign saying 'Private Woods Keep Out!" Mortimerry stared at Dunc, trying not to laugh. "No, no, Dunc! Private Woods doesn't mean that somebody with a surname called Woods was a private soldier in the film."

Flossie Jo tried to explain further. "It means... erm... It means that somebody owns all these trees... And that no one else is supposed to come in here."

"Yes," said Dunc, "especially a naughty man like Private Woods, who keeps wandering off when he should be acting like a soldier."

At this point Flossie Jo decided that no one could change Dunc's very strange mind. So she pointed at the last shed, and said, "Oh, let's go and see if anything's in there!"

But the heavy door was closed, and it took all of them to pull it open just enough to poke their heads in. After a few seconds their eyes got used to the dim light and they could see some metal boxes stacked against a wall.

Dunc was now feeling that he really should take charge of things. If the others were too silly to understand his explanation about Private Woods, they could hardly deal with things like, well, dangerous stuff. This was clearly a job for him, so he stepped forward and squeezed into the shed. He rubbed his fingers along the side of a dusty box, revealing some words printed on it. He pointed at each word and read them out, slowly and carefully, "Smoke... Canisters... Handle... With... Care."

Then, in his normal voice Dunc said, "Smoke canisters? That's interesting," and he lifted the lid off the box. Mortimerry, Onslow, Flossie Jo and Coco joined him, keen to see what he'd found.

The box was filled with grubby old cans about the size of a tin of baked beans. Dunc picked one up and passed it from hand to hand, concentrating hard.

"You wouldn't think smoke would be as heavy as this!" he said.

Mortimerry also reached down to pick up a can.

"Got it!" he exclaimed. "They're smoke bombs. I bet these were used by the actors in *Saving Private Ryan!*"

"Private Woods prob'ly used them too," said Dunc.

Mortimerry glanced at him but said nothing. He peered at the small letters printed on the can's label and read out the instructions. "One: Hold the canister at arm's length, away from your face. Two: Put your finger inside the red plastic ring."

The other Hobtails listened attentively as Mort went on.

"Three: Pull ring firmly upwards. Four: Place canister on ground. Five: Smoke will discharge within six seconds."

"Yep, done it!" said Dunc.

Mortimerry froze in shock... Then he spun round.

Dunc stood looking down. At his feet was a canister with the ring pulled up. Mortimerry stared in disbelief.

"Get out quick!" he screamed. "I was only reading the instructions. I didn't ask you to *do* anything!"

In a mad scramble, the Hobtails raced out of the

door. But poor Coco was still inside when the canister went 'POP! Hisssss…'.

In an instant, thick black smoke filled the little room. Coco staggered out, coughing and spluttering.

When they were at a safe distance they stopped to look back. At least, Mortimerry, Onslow, Flossie Jo and Dunc looked back; Coco was staring down at her pink dress, trying to brush off the black sooty stains.

"Oh, I knew I should have worn something dark today," she sobbed.

They could hardly see the little brick shed beneath the tower of smoke that rose up to the treetops.

"Who said you never get smoke without fire?" gasped Flossie Jo.

"Lucky for us there *was* no fire!" Mortimerry shouted, and he frowned at Dunc. "What were you thinking of? If those had been real bombs, *we* are the ones who would have gone up in smoke!"

Dunc looked quite offended. "What's your problem?

Nothing can go wrong if you follow the instructions on the can. Everyone knows that!"

From his perch high up on the control tower, Pellington saw the smoke rising from the woods. He immediately took flight and headed straight towards it.
"Hobtails!" he thought. "Something has happened. It always does!"
Pellington arrived within a minute and circled above the smoking shed to appraise the situation. He saw the young Hobtails arguing among themselves – which was something of a relief – and accounted for all five of them – which was a double relief!
He landed close by and asked, "Having a spot of bother, are we?" Onslow was quick to reply, "Nothing to worry about, honestly!"
Coco was aghast. "There's nothing to worry about *now,*" she replied, still wiping soot from her dress with a hankie.
Pellington coughed and used his wing to fan away some smoke from his face."Does anyone know you are here, so far from home?" he asked.
"Er, not exactly.... but there's no need to tell Gascoyne," pleaded Mortimerry. "He'll make us come home if he thinks we're getting into trouble."
Pellington was not totally convinced. "I would be failing in my duty if I did not report this incident to Gascoyne."
But Dunc protested, "Look, it was only a tin of smoke that went off! I'll show you." And he went to

14

get another canister.

"NO!" yelled Flossie Jo. "Just leave them alone!"

"Anyway," said Dunc, "it was all Mortimerry's fault."

The two Hobtails then began arguing again, pointing and accusing each other.

Nobody noticed Pellington fly off to deliver his report to Gascoyne, who, he presumed, would be busy tending the vegetables at his secret little garden in the Park.

"Alright," called Flossie Jo, "I've had enough of this arguing! I'm going to pick some blackberries. Nan Daisy needs them by lunchtime. Otherwise, there's no pie for dessert this evening!"

Dunc looked horrified, because he loved his food!

"Oh no, I forgot!" he wailed. "Nan Daisy's blackberry pie! Come on! Hurry up! We've got to go!"

Grabbing Mortimerry with one hand and Coco with the other, he hurried away after Flossie Jo, calling out to her, "Go to the garden in the old gamekeeper's cottage! That's where the best ones grow!"

Little Onslow trotted along behind, shouting, "Wait up! Wait for me!"

Chapter 2
THE OLD COTTAGE IN THE WOODS

The gamekeeper's cottage in Home Covert woods is very old and, once upon a time, it was very pretty, as Coco had remembered. But it had been empty for years. And now its roof, its floors and windows were broken, and a lot of work would need to be done to save it from falling apart. The garden was overgrown too, but the orchard there still provided lovely apples, pears and plums, which now only the woodland creatures and Hobtails ate.

The track that led to the house was also a terrible mess. In fact, with so many potholes, anthills and weeds on it, you'd hardly know it was a track fit for a car to drive on at all! That's why its owner, Farmer Beech, had to park his rickety old car quite a distance away when he went there with his family that very afternoon.

"Let's walk," he said to his wife, Mrs Beech.

"I wouldn't trust our car's suspension on those potholes. It will probably snap in half."

So he, his wife and their little daughter, Ellie, quietly strolled up the track towards the cottage. It also happened to be Ellie's birthday, and she was thinking about whether or not she could have a party.

As they walked, there was a sudden loud 'BANG!'

Mrs Beech jumped, and a flock of pigeons fluttered into the air from a nearby field. Farmer Beech took his wife's hand and smiled at her. She looked a bit embarrassed. "I think those wretched bird scarer things scare *me* more than the birds!" she said. "I never get used to them!"

"They scare me as well sometimes, and I put them there!" laughed her husband. "But I'd rather put up with those bangs than have the birds eat all the corn seed that we plant."

When the family arrived at the old house, they stood looking at it.

Mr Beech sighed. "My father would be sorry to see it in this bad state."

"Yes," said Mrs Beech. "I well remember him saying how much he liked coming here on summer evenings. But time marches on."

Mr Beech walked forward and touched one of the window frames. A strip of peeling paint fell to the ground. He shook his head. "You know, I hate having to sell this place. But, with our money problems, what else can we do?"

Mrs Beech nodded. "Is that man coming to see it

17

today?" she asked.

Ellie looked up at her dad.

"Yes," he said. "A chap called Grimes."

"Mmmm," her mother replied, doubtfully.

Ellie didn't like it when her parents were so serious like this – especially as it was her birthday – so she decided it would be nicer to go and play on the garden swing. And she skipped around the side of the house to see if it was still there...

The swing *was* there alright. But that wasn't the only thing she noticed when she came into the overgrown back garden. There were five strange 'children' staring at her. They had been picking blackberries, and one, in a very dirty pink dress, was sitting on the swing, eating some she had just collected.

Ellie immediately knew that these weren't proper children – like those at her school – although four of them were about the same size as her. They seemed to be as surprised by her as she was by them. But she wasn't afraid of them in the slightest. In fact she felt they were friendly. Then, the biggest of the blackberry pickers said, "Oh! Humans!" and disappeared into the bushes. But the others stayed exactly as they were when she arrived.

One said, "Hello. I'm Mortimerry."

The one in the dirty dress said, "Bonjour. I am Coco Legume."

Onslow said, "Hi. I'm Onslow, and that was Dunc who just went off." And the fourth one said, "My name's Flossie Jo. Who are you?"

18

Ellie said, "I'm Ellie. I came to play on the swing."

Coco got down from the swing. "Here you are then," she said. "It's your turn now."

Then some rustling and groaning from the bushes had them all looking around in wonder.

Now Hobtails are very tough, but even they can feel it when they get tangled up in thorny bramble bushes. So, when Dunc came crawling back into the garden, saying, "Ooh" and "Ahh" and "Ouch", Ellie was concerned.

"Are you alright? We've got some plasters at home."

Mortimerry laughed. "Don't worry. He'll be alright. He does this sort of thing all the time, but he never learns!"

The big Hobtail came over to meet Ellie, rubbing his sore arms and legs. "My name is Dunc. Do you want me to tell you about Private Woods?" he asked, hoping she would be interested. But, before she could answer, Flossie Jo said firmly, "No, Dunc, she doesn't, thank you very much!"

Ellie noticed the heart-shaped pattern on Flossie Jo's dungarees, and was puzzled by the 'H2H' written inside.

"It means we're 'Here to Help'," said Flossie Jo. "It's what we do."

"That's nice," replied Ellie with a smile and, as Coco held the seat steady for her, she climbed on to the swing.

The others went back to picking berries close by. But they were all still curious about the little girl who they'd just met. They watched as Coco stood behind Ellie and gave her a good push. And each time Ellie came back towards her, Coco pushed her again. Soon the little girl was swinging merrily backwards and forwards, to and fro.

Onslow smiled at Ellie. "We only came here to pick blackberries," he said.

"Yes," said Dunc, "our Nan Daisy makes the best blackberry pie you've ever tasted."

"Why did *you* come here?" Mortimerry asked.

And so Ellie began chatting away. For her age, she was a very good talker. In fact, Coco would say, later on, that she'd never heard such a small person say so much!

Ellie told the Hobtails that her full name was Ellie Amelia Beech, that she was six years old, and that today was her birthday.

Dunc immediately wished her "Happy birthday" and

gave her the six biggest blackberries in his can – one for every year of her age!

Ellie happily ate the berries – getting a lot of juice on her T-shirt as she did so.

The other Hobtails wished her a happy birthday too, and apologised for not having proper presents.

Ellie said that it was quite alright. "My Mummy says that it's the thought that counts."

She went on to tell them that she wanted to have a big birthday party – for all of the children in her class– but something had gone wrong at the bank and now her parents couldn't afford a party. She didn't mind though, because they promised her that once the old cottage was sold, they'd have some money. *Then* she could have a nice party!

Dunc was just starting to tell her about the best party he'd ever been to when they heard a lady's voice calling, "Ellie! Ellie! Where are you?"

It was Mrs Beech, who was walking around the side of the house.

Ellie looked around and felt a bit guilty. She said, "I'd better go. That's my Mummy."

Normally Ellie wouldn't have stayed away for more than a few minutes, so her Mummy just wanted to check on her. And when Mrs Beech thought she heard voices, she walked a little faster. But when she came into the back garden Ellie was all alone and swinging higher than her mother had ever seen her swing before.

Mrs Beech smiled. "I didn't know you could ride a swing on your own. What a clever girl you are!"

"Oh no, I couldn't do that on my own," Ellie replied. "My friend, Coco, was pushing me."

"Of course she was, darling," Mrs Beech murmured, looking around. "I should have known."

But when she went around the back of the swing to slow her down she noticed Coco's grubby hand marks on Ellie's shirt. Mrs Beech sounded surprised. "Where did all this smoky soot stuff come from?"

Ellie replied, "What soot?"

Chapter 3
Mr STONE and Mr GRIMES

The young Hobtails left the cottage garden and headed out of Home Covert woods. Each of their cans was now piled to the brim with juicy blackberries. They were walking along a dirt road that crossed a great field where winter wheat had been planted. Some pigeons were pecking about among the neat furrows, searching for seeds, and a couple of white butterflies danced together on the gentle breeze.

"You know, it's a pity about that little girl," Coco said. "I'd really like to give her a proper birthday present."

Dunc looked dreamy. "Yeah, a party too – with lots of good food!"

Suddenly, nearby, there was a loud 'BANG!'

Instantly, Dunc thought to protect his blackberries.

He clutched the can to his chest and threw himself to the ground and, as ever, a startled flock of pigeons took to the air and flew off into the woods. "I wish they wouldn't use those things," he growled, kneeling to collect a few berries that had spilled out. "They could just as easily shoot *us* instead of those birds!"

Mortimerry grinned. "There's nobody shooting at us, Dunc. Or the birds. It's only a gas gun. It just makes a noise to scare the birds away. Come and see."

Mort, Flossie Jo, Onslow and Coco left the track and walked into the field. Dunc followed, muttering. "I liked it better when they used scarecrows. At least you could talk to scarecrows – and they never tried to boss you about like some folk do," he said, staring hard at Coco.

The bird scarer was a simple-looking device. A gas bottle was connected by a tube to a box with a red metal pipe sticking out of it. At the back of the box was a switch pointing to 'Timer', which was set at ten minute intervals. Another could be switched from 'Low' to 'Loud'.

The timer switch could also be set to 'Manual' and had a green button next to it.

The cautious Hobtails stood a few paces away to study it. "Well, it looks like a gun. It's got a barrel like one," said Dunc.

"It is *not* a proper gun, and there are no bullets" replied Mortimerry. "It's a noise maker, that's all. Stand back. I'll show you."

Feeling a bit less brave than he seemed, Mortimerry

bent down for a closer look. But the others, feeling decidedly nervous, backed further away.

"Are you sure you know what you're doing?" asked Flossie Jo.

Mortimerry just nodded and rubbed his chin. He was pretty sure he knew what he was doing... but not totally sure.

"Yes, be careful!" advised Coco, while hiding behind Dunc. "And remember what happened to Talbot!"

Hearing her say that, they all paused to think about how the old, one-legged Hobtail came to lose his leg. But the funny thing was, none of them knew – because Talbot had never told anyone!

"I've switched it to 'Manual'," Mortimerry called. "Here we go..."

Then, as the others stuck their fingers in their ears, he pushed his thumb down on the green button.

There was a 'BANG!' so loud that Mortimerry toppled over and fell flat on his back. The others stood open mouthed in silence for a few moments.

Then Dunc chortled, "Pretty scary, eh, Mort?"

"Yes," giggled Onslow. "Scary even when you *know* it's not a real gun!"

A stunned Mortimerry sat up, looking confused. "Did somebody say something?" he said.

Flossie Jo gasped. "Oh dear, he can't hear us! That bang may have burst his eardrums!"

Mort's eyes were rolling and his head was spinning as he sat there, quite still, staring up at the sky.

Coco was getting worried and went to help him stand, but Flossie Jo said, "No, just leave him to recover. He's shell-shocked!"

Two minutes passed, but there was no change in his condition. Dunc looked at Mort's can of fruit on the ground and said, "I think I'll have a couple of his berries. He won't know, ha ha!" And went over to help himself.

"Oi!" said Mort, crossly. "You leave them alone! I'm alright now."

"Oh good," said Flossie Jo. "We've got to get out of here. It's too open in this field and we might be seen."

"But I wanted to come this way!" Dunc snapped, "'cos it's the quickest way home. And Nan Daisy needs these berries soon, while they're fresh, or she can't make us a pie."

"But there's nowhere to hide!" Flossie Jo explained.

"It's okay," said Mortimerry, still a bit dazed. "There's no one to see us... and the nearest footpath that humans use is half a mile away." But, as he said that, the sound of a diesel engine made them all turn round. A car was being driven in the next field. There were two men inside, and they were bouncing up and down on their seats as it moved along the bumpy track.

Coco gasped. "Oh no! It's coming this way!"

"RUN!" Flossie Jo shouted. With her free hand, she pulled Mortimerry to his feet and they raced away across the vast fifty acre field towards an old oak tree, which stood alone by a small pond.

As they ran, they all spilled some of their berries, but only Dunc stopped to gather his up.

"Don't be such a fool, Dunc!" Flossie Jo yelled. "Leave them! Come on!"

The Hobtails had seen the car when it was a long way off but, although they ran like the wind, Onslow and Dunc hadn't quite reached the tree when the car turned into their field.

There was a tall, thin man behind the steering wheel. This was Mr Stone, and his short, chubby

business partner, Mr Grimes, sat in the back. They always referred to themselves as 'Mr', to give others the impression they were polite and respectable people. The men were on there way to meet a poor farmer.

However, Mr Grimes was constantly moaning as he jerked and bounced about on his seat. But when he saw two little figures disappearing behind a distant oak tree, he sat up straight and his eyes opened wide. "Did you see that?" he said, his voice full of surprise.

"See what?" asked Mr Stone, who was too busy watching the bumpy track to notice anything else.

"Something odd. Some little creatures... two of them... ran behind that tree," said Mr. Grimes, getting more and more excited.

"Probably just kids playing," replied Mr Stone.

"They didn't move like kids!" shouted Mr Grimes. "And were probably up to no good, and now trying to hide..They could even be hiding from *us*! But why?"

Mr Stone rolled his eyes and looked weary. "So... they're hiding! Kids like to hide! What d'you want me to do about it?"

"I want you to drive over there so I can find out what's going on..."

Shaking his head and looking grumpy, Mr Stone said, "Alright. No need to get upset!"

Changing down to second gear he drove the big black car off the track and through a field towards the tree. Even at a slow five miles per hour, the car bumped up and down and swayed from side to side – even worse than before. But Mr Grimes didn't care.

"If we are to buy out this farmer," he shouted, "I want to know what's going on around these parts! I don't want any strange business happening on my patch! And what I just saw looked *very* strange indeed!"

Although the tree in the field seemed like any other old tree, it was actually the oldest around. It still had leaves on some of its branches, but much of the bark had fallen off its trunk and it was hollow.

Little Onslow remembered what Gascoyne, the Hobtails' leader, had once told him: "Never draw attention to that tree! Mark my words, young 'un! If humans was to find what's in yon trunk, they'd be choppin' down every old tree in the county!"

Gascoyne had also warned them all before to stay away from it, lest it got damaged. He always called it 'Bessie's Oak', although the young Hobtails had forgotten why. And, normally, these youngsters would *not* go near it for other reasons too – because heavy branches could drop off a dying tree and the whole thing could fall down at any time and, what's more, a single tree standing alone in a field can attract dangerous lightning bolts during thunderstorms.

Onslow was just about to mention what Gascoyne had told him when there was a loud thud. Mortimerry said, "Shhhh!" and they listened hard. The noise was made by the approaching car as it dipped in and out of a large hole, making the car rock violently. This sent Mr Stone lurching forward, and his forehead banged on the centre of the steering wheel, setting off the horn with a long 'beeeeep'. This served as an alarm call to

29

the Hobtails and they scrambled down through a large rabbit hole that, fortunately, entered the hollow tree. Dunc – the last one in – dragged twigs and fallen leaves behind him to block up the hole.

Mr Stone had now had enough. He slammed his foot on the brakes, and the car bounced to a halt about thirty yards from the tree where the Hobtails hid.

While Mr Stone rubbed his sore head, Mr Grimes threw the car door open and leaped out, waving his rolled-up umbrella. He shouted, "I know you're here. Show yourselves you young scoundrels!" But then he tripped on a fallen branch and almost toppled into the pond there. By the time he'd picked himself up and straightened his tie, Mr Stone had joined him.

"Where are they then?" Stone asked. "I don't see any strange little people!"

"They must be hiding here somewhere!" said Grimes, looking at the pond. " They can't fool me!"

Balancing as best he could, the overweight Mr. Grimes hurried up the slope toward the tree. Then he stood there, wiping his sweaty forehead with a handkerchief, searching all about with his small, piggy eyes.

Mr Stone smirked as he came to stand beside him. "Well, well! That is *very* odd alright! They're either in the pond or they've disappeared into thin air! What are they? Mermaids or ghosts?"

"Don't you be cheeky with me!" shouted Grimes. "I know what I saw. They must be here somewhere. And I don't like it. The public are not allowed to be

30

here, either. This is private land."

The two men stood together at the bottom of the old tree, looking it up and down. They walked around the trunk, in opposite directions, so nothing could escape being seen. Last year's dry brown leaves were piled around the base, and as Grimes rustled through them, his leg suddenly sank down into a hole, up to his knee. He didn't know it, but his foot was jammed hard against Dunc's leg, nearly making the poor Hobtail yell with pain.

Grimes snarled, "Drat! I'm stuck. Get me out! Get.. me... OUT! This place is bewitched!"

Stone stood behind his helpless, struggling business partner. He enjoyed seeing him become so distressed because it made *him* feel more powerful – for once.

"Help! Where are you?" ranted Grimes. "Am I to stay here forever?"

"Now there's an idea!" thought Stone, quietly wondering if he should leave him there to perish. His scheming mind realised that, without his partner, he could buy the cottage and woodland for himself. And he could make loads of money – and keep the lot.

Stone also realised that nobody but he knew where the unfortunate Mr Grimes was going that day, as he had no wife or children either. It could be weeks before he was found...

Grimes' cries for help were getting louder and more desperate. "Where are you? Pleeeease, get me out!" he squealed.

Dunc was getting desperate too. His leg was hurting and he wondered if he'd been trapped deliberately.

Stone's grubby mind was now racing with the possibilities of wealth.... power... and prison! Eventually it occurred to him that Grimes could be found sooner rather than later and, what's worse, he could be found alive! So, reluctantly, he decided to help. "Oh there you are, my poor friend!" said Stone. "I came as quickly as I could." Then, having said that, he grabbed his snivelling partner under the armpits and heaved him out of the hole.

The two men stood there for a moment, wrapped in each other's arms, as though they were cuddling. But, as the tall man tried to wriggle free, Grimes' eyes fell upon some distant woods – a sight that had him transfixed with excitement – and he clutched the tall man even tighter "Now *that's* what I call bewitching!" he said. "Let me go, I can't breathe!" gasped Stone.

"Oh, oh, I am sorry," replied Grimes, releasing his rescuer. "My mind was elsewhere."

The very thought of making money had made him forget about the hole his foot had gone down... and forgotten too were the strange little creatures he'd seen. But, if he *had* thought about it, he may have realised where they were hiding.....And listening!

"If you would care to look to your right, my dear Mr Stone, you will see the beautiful Home Covert woodland. And after our meeting at the cottage, I will show you around the woods and our new plans for it. Ha Ha! Those *poor* weeping willow trees will be crying real tears after we've sent in the woodchoppers" said a jubilant Mr Grimes.

Then Coco whispered to the others, "I think those men are talking about the gamekeepers cottage and the woods that belong to Ellie's family."

Chapter 4
MAKING PLANS

The five Hobtails were crammed quietly, but uncomfortably, inside the hollow tree. Dunc, at the bottom, was rubbing his bruised leg, and he had Onslow's knee digging him in the ear too. Mortimerry was wedged above Onslow, Flossie Jo was sitting on Mort's head, and, finally, Coco was at the top of the pile, standing on Flossie Jo's shoulders. She was staring out through a woodpecker's hole, and saw the two men return to their vehicle.

She watched as Mr Grimes unrolled a big architect's drawing and laid it over the bonnet of the car. The two men were pointing at the drawing, then pointing at the woods. She could still hear parts of their conversation, and repeated what she could hear to the others.

"We should keep the shape," Grimes said, grandly. "A circle of trees around an estate always looks well. But all the other trees will go, and we'll knock down that old gamekeeper's cottage too. We'll be able to get four big new houses in its back garden alone."

This idea pleased Stone greatly. He rubbed his hands together and grinned. "We could easily fit a hundred houses in those woods! Of course, we won't call them plain 'houses'. We'll call them 'luxury residences in a mature woodland setting'. And we, my friend, are going to be rich. Hee, hee!"

Grimes was laughing too as he rolled up the drawings, but something suddenly concerned Stone. The smile left his face and he said, in a serious voice, "You haven't told this fellow... What's his name?... Farmer Beech... about our plans for the housing estate?"

"Certainly not!" laughed Mr Grimes. "He's a real country bumpkin! He wants to keep everything the same as it always was. Stupid man! So, until he sells it all to us... we'll let him believe that I'm going to repair the old ruin... and live in it myself with my family! He won't realise the nature of our little game"

The two men chuckled out loud and shook hands vigorously.

"I say, old chap," said Grimes,"that wreck of a cottage has given *me* an idea for a game. Hide-and-seek. We take the cottage and woods away, then – later – he can try to find them! Ha ha!"

The men were completely unaware that others could hear their conversation.

"Did you hear that?" Coco whispered. "Those rotters are going to trick Ellie's father! We've got to stop them!" The rest of the Hobtail gang whispered back their agreement – except Dunc, who didn't reply because blackberries were falling down, one by one, from somebody's can. And he was too busy stretching out his tongue trying to catch them!

Outside, Mr Grimes and Mr Stone climbed into their car and returned to the farm track that led to the cottage in the woods.

When the sound of the engine died away, Mortimerry said, "Alright, Dunc, let's get out of here."

After a few seconds of him squirming and grunting, the leaves and twigs in the rabbit hole began to move and Dunc slowly emerged feet first. "Phew!" he gasped, wiping blackberry juice and mud from his face. "I wouldn't like to live in a tree house. They're too cramped!"

Coco was the last one left inside the tree trunk but, as she was about to leave, she noticed something shiny on the ground. A beam of sunlight, shining down through the woodpecker's hole had lit up something that was truly amazing.

Just a few inches in front of her, lying in the loose soil that rabbits had dug up, was a necklace with a gold pendant. She picked it up and rubbed it on her skirt to get the dirt off. She held it up towards the light and saw sparkling glassy colours: reds, whites and blues.

"Hurry up, Coco!" Flossie Jo shouted into the hole. "We've got to help Ellie. Come on!"

But Coco was too interested in the necklace and didn't reply. Nor did she reply the second time she

36

was called. So Flossie Jo crawled back into the hollow tree to get her.

"*What* is keeping you?" she said, angrily.

"Decisions, decisions," said Coco, putting the chain over her head. "I've just found this pretty necklace that a rabbit has kindly dug up. Do you think it suits me?"

Flossie Jo squinted to see in the semi-darkness. She could barely make out the shape of the pendant – and she also had more important things to consider. But to keep Coco happy, she said, "Yes, it suits you fine. Now hurry up, my little princess, we've got to tell Ellie about those two crooks."

As Coco went to take off the necklace, she stopped halfway. "Er, what shall I do with it?" she asked.

"Oh.... just keep it!" said Flossie Jo, impatiently. "It must have been in the ground for ages. It can't belong to anyone now."

At long last, Flossie Jo managed to get Coco out of the tree. And as soon as they both emerged, Mortimerry, Dunc and Onslow began running off toward the woods.

"Come on, you two!" Mort shouted.

Coco tucked the necklace inside the front of her dress to stop it flapping about, then chased after them.

Chapter 5
THINGS AREN'T WHAT THEY SEEM

Eventually, Mr Grimes and Mr Stone arrived at the woods. They parked their car and walked towards the gamekeeper's cottage. Farmer Beech greeted them at the garden gate and shook their hands.

"Very pleased to meet you, at last, Farmer Beech," said Mr. Grimes, cheerfully.

"And this is Mr Stone, an expert builder, who specialises in restoring the charm to lovely old cottages such as yours."

"Oh, good!" said Farmer Beech, "And I'm pleased to meet you, sir."

Then Mr Grimes asked, "Have you had a good harvest?"

Farmer Beech shook his head. "No, it's been a bad year again, I'm afraid."

Mr Grimes put on a sad face. "Oh, I am so sorry to hear that," he lied.

Then Grimes and Stone were introduced to Mrs Beech. She was polite to them both, but not too friendly – because there was something about them she didn't trust. Little Ellie just hid behind her mother's skirt, peering up at the two strangers.

"So, this will be my new family home," said Mr Grimes, pretending to be impressed by the tatty old house.

"Well, take it as you find it," said Farmer Beech, trying hard to sound cheerful. "Of course, it has seen better days, but I'm sure it can be restored to its former glory. Do you know, it was built in 1788 by my great grandfather's great grandfather..."

And he went on to tell the history of the house and how it was passed down from father to son.

Mr Grimes and Mr Stone seemed to listen with interest. They said things like, "Gosh!" and "Well, can you believe that?" and "How lovely it must have been!" But, as they viewed the cottage, Mr Stone also said things like, "Oh dear, it will need a new roof..." and "The doors and window frames have got woodworm..." and "This will be very expensive to fix..."

Mrs Beech and Ellie stood quietly, watching them.

Meanwhile, in the overgrown garden at the back of the house, the Hobtails appeared from out of the bushes. Mortimerry pointed at an old wheelbarrow with a flat tyre. "Let's leave our berries here, where we can find them."

But Dunc held on to his can. He said, "I don't want to leave mine! You've dropped most of yours. I want to make sure Nan Daisy can make a pie for supper - at least one for me!"

"Dunc!" snapped Flossie Jo, "will you please stop worrying about food?"

"Yes," added Mortimerry. He was cross too, but kept his voice low. "What's more important? Saving blackberries or saving Ellie's family from crooks?" Then he mumbled,"Although I'm not sure how!"

"And don't forget," said Onslow, "*we'll* be saving the orchard *and* the old house too!"

Dunc lowered his gaze and tutted. He was a bit upset, but when the others put down their cans of fruit he reluctantly did the same, although he insisted on putting his can just a bit away from the other ones – so there could be no mix up later.

Without another word, they all ran off around the side of the cottage. But a few seconds later Dunc was back. He scooped a handful of berries from his can and stuffed them into his mouth. Then, with dark red juice dribbling from his lips, he hurried back after the others.

At the front of the house, Farmer Beech was explaining his reluctance to sell. "To be honest with you," he said to Mr Grimes and Mr Stone, "I'd never think of selling it, if it wasn't for the little money we earn now. Seed, fuel and tractors are very expensive these days and, apart from that, we can't always sell the crops that we do manage to grow."

As he went on talking, none of them, not even Ellie, noticed the Hobtails coming through the trees towards the garden. They moved as silently as ghosts and, within a few moments, Mortimerry, Onslow, Flossie Jo, Coco and Dunc were hidden in a dense privet hedge, just a few feet away from the humans. They crouched there, listening to every word.

Mr Grimes had talked with farmers before. He knew that once they started on about their problems they could talk for hours. So, determined to cut the conversation short, he interrupted. "Oh, excuse me, Mr Beech, but you never introduced us to this sweet young girl."

The farmer smiled proudly and said, "Oh, I'm sorry. This is our daughter, Ellie."

Grimes stooped down and shook Ellie's little hand with his soft, chubby fist.

There was something about his smile that reminded Ellie of her uncle's prized pig. And Mr Stone reminded her of his skinny old goat! "Well, young Ellie," Grimes said, "I know that you'll have a lovely time playing with my daughter Susan when we come to live here." Mrs Beech was confused. "My husband said your daughter's name is Mary!" And this confused Mr Grimes too for a moment, as he struggled to think of an answer. Mr Stone came to his rescue. "Oh, but he has *two* darling daughters," he said.

"Yes, yes!" laughed Mr Grimes. "How could I forget? Susan *and* Mary. And the little dears are so much looking forward to riding their ponies through the woodland paths," he said, gesturing at the trees.

The group came to a small outbuilding in a corner of the garden. Mr Stone went to look inside. He picked up a metal bucket that was in his way and passed it to Mr Grimes, telling him, "This shed will be useful. You'll be able to keep your lawn mower and bicycles in here."

Mrs Beech laughed. "There won't be enough room. This is the cottage toilet. There isn't one indoors!"

"What? An outside toilet!" said a startled Mr Stone.

"Yes. I thought you were an expert!" replied Mrs Beech. "What did you expect to find in a very old cottage out here in the woods?"

"Where, er, *is* the loo, then?" asked Mr Stone, looking around.

"Your friend is holding it," said Mrs Beech, trying not to laugh.

"Urrrrgh," gulped Mr Grimes, dropping the bucket immediately. Mrs Beech reassured him. "Don't worry. Nobody has sat on it for years!"

Then a thought came to Grimes. "Well, what happens if I need the toilet in the middle of the night... and it's raining?" he said. "Then you'll have to take a torch and an umbrella!" replied Mrs Beech. "And, before you ask," she continued, "there is no electricity either, and you get your water from a well not too far from here."

The two men stared blankly at the toilet bucket rolling on the grass. They hadn't thought about such things as water, electricity and toilets before!

"Silly me," said Grimes, trying to compose himself. "Who needs modern conveniences anyway?"

"So," said the farmer, "you're sure you want to buy the woods as well?"

"Oh yes! I am indeed, Mr Beech. I could not buy the one thing without the other. My wife and I greatly value our privacy. We are just simple country folk at heart. We want peace and quiet. Unspoiled nature. That's the thing for us."

The farmer nodded. "Yes, they're the things that we like too."

"And," Grimes continued, "we couldn't stand the idea that, one day, you might sell off the woods to some people who'd chop down all the trees for firewood... or something."

From inside the hedge the Hobtails glanced at one another. They were surprised and angry.

"Why is he saying that?" Dunc whispered. "That's not what he said before!"

"He's telling lies," whispered Mortimerry. "Because he is a liar!"

"A liar?" whispered Dunc, deeply shocked. "That's really, really bad!"

Farmer Beech looked at his wife, seeking her support. She nodded her agreement and hung her head.

"Well, if we can agree a fair price, I suppose we can sell the woods too. But, don't you want to take a look at the inside of the cottage first, before making a final decision?"

"Yes, yes, of course," said Mr Grimes. "You're absolutely right."

Mr Stone nodded, and took out a pencil and notebook.

Grimes pretended to be very excited. "I am so looking forward to this! A guided tour of the house! Please lead on," he said, even though he was planning to knock it down.

So, Mr Beech unlocked the front door and turned the handle. It opened with a great, slow creak. One by one they all stepped inside, brushing away hanging cobwebs as they went.

But – still hidden in the hedge – the Hobtails were outraged.

"This is very, very awful!" said Coco.

"Those men are such liars!" said Dunc. "Somebody should punish them!"

"Like how?" asked Flossie.

"Erm...No dinner for two days," replied Dunc.

Onslow suggested the worst thing would be having to go to bed early for a week. But Coco thought not being allowed to play with her dressing up clothes would be worse still.

Mortimerry shook his head. "I doubt if any of those punishments would bother the men, but we've got to do something."

"Yes." replied Flossie Jo, "Something that will make

them go away, and stay away!'"

Dunc suggested, "We could write on the windscreen of their car: 'Big... Liars... Go... Away!'"

This gave Flossie Jo an idea, and she sort of agreed. "Dunc's got a point. There are quite a few old signs around here saying 'Danger' and 'Keep Out' which might put them off a bit."

Dunc smiled; he was pleased that he was being taken seriously for once. "Yes, and I know where there's some really frightening signs," he said. "Ones that were probably put up to scare that Private Woods soldier. I'll go and get them." And he trotted off enthusiastically. But Mortimerry remained doubtful. "It's worth a try," he said, "but I don't think signs alone will scare those men enough..."

Coco looked at her sooty dress. "Oh yes!" she said, raising her eyes at the memory, "Talking of scary things, that smoke bomb and that bird scarer thing didn't half give me a fright!"

Mort and Flossie Jo stared at one another. The same idea came to them at the same moment.

"Brilliant!" said Mort. "Why didn't I think of it earlier?"

"What a scary combination!" exclaimed Flossie Jo. "Smoke bombs, gas guns *and* danger signs!"

Mortimerry clapped his hands together. "Come on then! I'm sure Mr Beech won't mind us borrowing his equipment," he said, pointing over to the fields.

"Let's prepare a surprise party for our special guests, Mr Grimes and Mr Stone."

So, while Mort and Coco jogged away to collect the gas guns, Flossie and Onslow went back to the brick sheds to get the smoke canisters. "This is going to be a very *unpleasant* surprise party too!" she thought.

Chapter 6
SURPRISE GARDEN PARTY

Inside the gamekeeper's cottage Mr Stone went around measuring the doors, windows and fireplaces. He appeared to be writing the results in his notebook – but he was only making scribbles.

Mr Grimes walked about the rooms with Mr and Mrs Beech. They were telling him who was who in the faded family photos and recalling where different pieces of furniture came from. Mr Grimes encouraged them by saying such things as, "Oh, we must preserve this!" or, "What splendid craftsmanship!" but, when the Beeches went off into another room, Mr Grimes muttered to Mr Stone, "What a dump! I wouldn't keep pigs in here!"

Half an hour later they came out of the cottage and Farmer Beech locked the door. "We must be off home now," he said. "There is always work to do on a farm, you know."

"Excellent," said Mr. Grimes. "Now, you think about the offer I've made… and I'm sure you'll agree that it's a fair one…" Then his eyes narrowed. He took some folded ten pound notes from his pocket, and put them into Mr Beech's hand.

"Here you are. A non-returnable cash deposit for you, to prove I mean business. And tomorrow, when you sign the contract, my friend, much, much more will be yours."

The farmer looked at the paper money and thought

to himself, "That's not even enough to pay for Ellie's party!" But, as he turned to walk away, he noticed that Mr Grimes and Mr Stone were not following him.

He looked back and said, "Aren't *you* leaving as well? Is there something else you need to see?"

Mr Grimes smiled pleasantly. "Nothing you need to bother yourself about, Mr Beech. But, if it's alright with you, I'd like to take a stroll through the woods... to familiarise myself with the sunlit paths... and to see, at first hand, the varied, flora and er... er, what's the other thing?" said Grimes, turning to his colleague.

"Fauna," said Mr Stone, helpfully. "Flora and fauna. Flowers and animals, you know. That sort of thing."

Mrs Beech frowned. "Yes, we do know. We are *farmers!*"

Mr Beech just nodded, and said, "Well, enjoy your stroll, gentlemen. And we'll see you tomorrow."

Dunc peeped around the corner of the house, then made a signal to the other Hobtails behind him. They quickly disappeared, moments before the two crooks walked into the back garden, both looking very smug and pleased with themselves.

"That was clever of you,"said Mr Stone. "The varied 'flora and fauna' indeed! Ha ha!"

"Yes, even if I do say so myself," Grimes replied, "he fell for that one! As if I care about flowers and animals! I don't know anything about them. But I *do* know we could make more money selling the trees here for timber than we'll be paying the farmer for all of this land; he really doesn't know what it's worth!"

Stone raised his hat. "A good bit of business, dear friend. For us, anyway!" he sneered.

The men searched along the dense bushes and hedges that enclosed the garden, looking for a way out. And they still had big smiles on their faces as they approached the back gate that led to the woods.

"Oh, I do love it when a plan comes together!" said a gleeful Grimes.

"Me too," sniggered Stone.

"Yes, and so do I," whispered Mortimerry, who was hiding with one of the bird scarer gas guns just a few feet away.

Across the path from him, Flossie Jo and Coco lay in wait with a box of smoke canisters. And on the other side of the garden, Dunc and Onslow were hiding with their bird scarer, itching to start.

Stone tried to open the back gate, but it was locked

and too high for the men to climb over. Grimes tore away some ivy and peeped through into the woods.

"What's that?" he asked, sounding worried.

Then Stone had a look and replied sarcastically, "It's an old wooden sign saying 'Private Woods. Keep Out'. That's all."

Grimes made a bigger hole in the ivy for a better look. "But… but…," he said, in a most serious tone, "there are signs all around the place…"

And, sure enough, in every direction they looked, there were signs stuck in the earth or fixed on trees. The men didn't understand exactly what they referred to but they all said the same sort of thing: 'Danger to Life'. 'Unsafe Ground'. 'No Trespassing'. 'Guard Dog Patrols'. 'Strictly No Entry'. 'Do Not Pass This Point'. 'Beware Sudden Noises'. 'Keep Out!'

"We could've walked into a minefield out there!" gulped Grimes.

"Don't be such a nervous nelly!" snapped Stone. He pointed back the way they had come. "Look, the old De Havilland aeroplane factory was just over there. After the war the soldiers guarding the place probably dumped all kinds of junk in these woods, including those old signs."

"I know, and that's my point!" a shaky Grimes replied. "Because bombs *were* dropped on the factory, any unexploded ones could've been dumped here. And an old bomb will blow you to bits just as well as a new one!" But Stone growled back, "Who cares? It won't be *us* that lives here!"

It was clearly time for the party to begin. Mortimerry switched his borrowed gas gun to 'Manual' and set the other knob to 'Loud'. Then, Flossie Jo pulled back the red plastic ring on a smoke canister. "Six seconds," She whispered, and Mortimerry started his countdown, "6... 5... 4... " Flossie lobbed the canister over the garden hedge towards the businessmen.

It came to a silent stop just behind Mr Stone.

Grimes' worries had made Stone really cross. "Listen to me, man! All those wartime bombs were made harmless years and years ago! There's nothing to worry about now."

Mortimerry finished his countdown. "3...2... 1... Here we go!" he said, and stuck his fingers in his ears – he was fully prepared this time! He stretched out a leg and pressed the green button with his foot...

There was a deafening 'BANG!' and, at the same time, thick, dark smoke belched up from behind Mr Stone, blotting out the light. A flock of pigeons in the trees above flapped wildly among the branches, causing a few lost feathers to float slowly down.

The partners were now in a panic. They'd lost sight of each other and staggered around the garden, blinded in the black fog. They ran this way and that way – and collided without recognising each other!

Stone scampered away, whimpering, "Don't shoot, whoever you are! I surrender!"

While Grimes begged, "Have mercy, pleeease! I'm too young to die!"

Through the murky fog, Grimes caught a glimpse of daylight and he stumbled towards it. But, as he stopped briefly to rub his watering eyes, Onslow let off his first smoke canister, which obscured the light with another dark cloud. There seemed no escape.

It was now Dunc's turn, and he was ready and waiting by his bird scarer. As arranged, he'd counted to ten after Mort's opening blast, then brought his foot down on the green button. Another bomb-sized explosion echoed through the trees.

The desperate Grimes called out to Stone by his first name, "Arthur, old chap, where are you? Talk to me!"

Stone was just about to reply, "Over here, Basil!" when his knee banged into a wheelbarrow, which tipped forward and knocked over Dunc's can of blackberries. As Stone hopped around, rubbing his painful knee, his size 12 right foot squashed every last berry.

Dunc saw this and howled with rage. His deep roar of frustration adding an eerie element to the proceedings. For good measure, Coco tossed another canister over the garden hedge and more smoke billowed forth. Mortimerry complemented this by discharging one more noisy blank from his gas gun, panicking the crooks further into blindly running 'hither and thither' as Nan Daisy would say.

Stone dashed through the swirling blackness and clattered, face first, straight into the 'For Sale' sign. "Oh! My poor nose!" he wailed.

Both men were terrified and feared for their lives. Neither of them could tell if they were coming or going. They frantically fumbled their way around the garden hedge, getting their fingers pricked by thorns as they tried to find a way out. For the second time they crashed into one another and collapsed, a few paces apart.

Recognising the familiar sound of the other's moans and groans, the men called out, breathlessly and in hope.

"Stone, is that you?"

"Grimes?"

"Basil!"

"Oh, Arthur!"

The partners crawled closer. They had never been so pleased to see each other.

"No wonder that farmer was selling all this so cheap! It's a death trap!" said Stone. "He's taken our deposit money and lured us here to be slaughtered!"

Grimes agreed. "Yes. This place is jinxed. And I bet he's got those strange little creatures I saw, helping him!"

"Oh, not again!" grumbled Stone. "Our lives are in danger and you keep on about 'little creatures'. Just forget them. They only exist in your tiny, little mind!"

"How dare you say that!" Grimes snivelled. "It's your fault we're in this mess. And we'll never get our deposit money back now!"

Stone was furious. "Okay, if that's what you think," he said. "Let's see how you get along on your own! Our partnership is finished! It's every man for himself now!"

Grimes grabbed him by the sleeve and spoke softly, like he was a wounded soldier in a film. "Alright, but if *you* manage to make it back... and I don't... please tell my wife and children that I love them."

Stone spluttered, "You fool! You haven't even got a family! Remember?"

Their chance meeting was brought to a swift end when Flossie Jo's last smoke canister came over the hedge and rolled between them. They thought it was a stick of dynamite and quickly scrambled away in horror – once again losing sight of each other in the large garden.

Coco, meanwhile, was having a little rest. She was sitting on a log outside the front garden gate, calmly listening to the bangs and screams, when another deafening explosion from Dunc's gas gun had the effect of driving the former business partners towards her. Stone got lucky. He came across the gate which Coco had left open, and fled out into the field looking for his car.

"My goodness!" thought Coco, smiling to herself. "That man *does* look in a hurry!"

Grimes, though, wasn't as fortunate. When he ran past the outside loo building, he didn't see the toilet bucket that he'd dropped earlier – and trod in it. His foot got jammed in so tightly that he couldn't shake it off, and so, coughing and wheezing, he hobbled away, still vainly searching for an exit.

Next, he blundered into the old gamekeeper's cottage, but found the doors were locked. But when he saw the path, he remembered it led to the field, and he staggered down it, clonking along with the bucket still firmly attached to his foot.

When he found the front gate wide open he whinnied with joy and limped through it as fast as he could... but he skidded to a halt when he came face to face with Coco.

As Grimes viewed the strange little creature in front of him, his eyes widened and his jaw dropped. "Don't hurt me!" he sobbed. "You can keep the woods... and the cottage. I don't want them anymore!"

He began to edge away from her, backwards through the gate. Then he closed it for his own protection and staggered straight back into the smoke-filled garden, wondering if he was going mad!

However, less than a mile away, the Beeches' car was at the end of the track and about to join the main road, when Mrs Beech said, "Do you know, I think there's something wrong with those bird scarer gas gun things. The timing sounds all wrong."

Mr Beech stopped the car and wound down his window. He could hear the distant bangs. They were definitely going off much too quickly – and sometimes only ten seconds apart! "I'd better go and fix them," he said.

But when Mrs Beech and Ellie looked back, they gasped at the sight of smoke rising above the woods.

"The cottage is on fire!" cried Ellie.

"Oh, my goodness!" exclaimed her father. He quickly reversed the car and drove back the way they'd come.

Mr Beech was now very worried. "If the cottage

burns down, Mr Grimes won't want to buy it! Nor will anyone else!"

Although he was forced into selling the woods and the cottage, he would always care about them because they had meant so much to his family. And he secretly wished that he was able to repair the old place himself. But the sad thing was, he just didn't have the money to do it. His wife knew what he was thinking too. She stroked his arm. "Don't worry, dear," she said, "if it has burnt down, we will manage somehow. We always do!"

Chapter 7
A PARTING SHOT

Back in the woods, Dunc and Onslow moved their gas gun to a new position just outside the garden, and triggered another blast. Mortimerry detected that the pitiful "Aaarrggghhh!" that followed was now the wailing of only *one* man.

"Game over... and cease fire!" he said to Flossie Jo, and whistled for the other Hobtails to join him.

Within a few minutes the smoke had begun to drift away, allowing Grimes to see a small gap under the hedge, through which he made an undignified, scrambling exit. He was too scared of Coco to approach the front gate, and she watched with interest as he splashed across a ditch full of stagnant water, then crawled through a barbed wire fence. And she giggled when a sharp barb ripped away a big patch from the seat of his trousers, exposing his bare bottom! "Serves him right!" she thought.

Peace was now restored at the old gamekeeper's cottage, but the cause and effect of the explosions had seemed so realistic that Coco imagined she'd been part of a dramatic battle scene from a war film – maybe one like *Saving Private Ryan*, for all she knew. But here – as in films – nobody got hurt and there wasn't any real damage.

Nevertheless, the two men had become terrified! As the tall, thin Stone sprinted across the field, the chubby little Grimes limped and hopped after him, calling, "Wait for me! Wait for me!"

Mortimerry leaned on a fence post, smiling. "Well, I must say, *that* worked a treat!" he said.

"Yes, that was fun," said Onslow.

"Fun for us, maybe," Flossie Jo laughed. "But not for them!"

"Come on, everybody," said Mort, "let's have a clear-up and get these gas guns back where they belong."

When Mr Stone arrived back at his car he immediately started the engine. He didn't care that Grimes was begging him to wait, and, without a backward glance, he drove off down the bumpy track.

Mr Grimes stopped and shouted, "You heartless brute! How could you abandon a comrade during the heat of battle?"

He was now feeling very sorry for himself indeed. He was dirtied by soot, soaked by ditch water, smelled like a sewer – and he still had a rusty toilet bucket stuck on his foot! It was just then that he felt a cold draught of air on his bare bottom, and realised that his trousers were badly torn. He was too miserable to be embarrassed by then, and trudged along the track bemoaning his bad luck.

But, shortly after leaving, Stone had to stop his car again as Farmer Beech's car appeared, coming towards him, around a bend in the bumpy road. Both men had to brake sharply to avoid a collision. Stone beep-beep-beeped on his horn. "Get out of my way!" he yelled, angrily.

"What on earth's the matter?" replied Mr Beech. "Calm down!" said his wife. "We have Ellie with us!"

Grimes saw his chance to catch up. He finally shook the bucket off his foot and – with renewed hope – ran towards the cars.

As the two drivers slowly squeezed their vehicles past one another in the narrow space, Stone shouted at the farmer, "You nearly killed us!"

At that moment Grimes arrived. He jumped into

Stone's car and joined in the argument. "You tried to trick us into buying that highly dangerous property!" he roared.

"I really don't know what you're talking about," replied Mr Beech.

"Don't lie to us! That place should be condemned!" Stone ranted.

"Yes. And the deal is off! Goodbye and good riddance!" spouted Grimes.

And with that, Stone pressed hard on the accelerator and his car sped away, bumping and swaying down the track, never to return.

"Charming!" said Mrs Beech. "What awful men!"
A rather shocked Mr Beech decided he'd better hurry to the old cottage to see what state it was in.
Mrs Beech pointed out that she couldn't see smoke anymore. "Maybe the cottage has burnt to the ground!" she said.

"It can't have!" replied her husband. "We only left there about ten minutes ago!"

Ellie had tears in her eyes. "Those men had better not have hurt the cottage," she sniffed.
And when they arrived, she was first out of the car and ran ahead to have a look.

A few moments later she called out, excitedly. "Mummy! Daddy! The cottage is alright! Nothing is on fire!"

Her parents were speechless as they stood on the path, staring at the old building. Both were confused, because it was just how they'd left it. The whole family was beginning to feel a lot more cheerful too.

Mrs Beech put her arm round her husband. "I'm so happy those men have gone and the cottage wasn't sold," she said.

Farmer Beech nodded and cuddled his wife and daughter. "Some guardian angel was taking care of us today," he replied, looking around the garden for a clue.

But, as he spoke, Mrs Beech noticed a mysterious chalk drawing on the front door. It was heart shaped, with 'H2H' written inside. Pointing at it, she said, "That wasn't there before! I wonder what it means?" Ellie was quick to answer. "Here to help," she said, with a smile. "Flossie Jo probably did it."

Her father was baffled. "Who is Flossie Jo?" he asked.

"Oh, just one of her imaginary friends," laughed Mrs Beech. "Now, Ellie, as it's your birthday, why don't you have a play on the swing while Daddy and I check the inside of the cottage?"

So Ellie skipped across the garden to the swing. When she got there her eyes lit up, because the words 'Happy Birthday' had been chalked upon the seat.

Suddenly, a voice, in hushed tones, called out to her, "Psst, Ellie, we're over here!"

It was Coco, standing behind the locked back gate.

Ellie trotted over, delighted to see her there with Dunc, Flossie Jo, Onslow and Mortimerry.

"Those horrible men have gone," said Ellie.

"We know," replied Flossie.

"Sorry, but we can't come in to play," said Mortimerry, "'cos it's getting late. But we just wanted to say goodbye before we went home."
Then, Onslow and Dunc sang in a whisper, "Happy birthday, dear Ellie, happy birthday to you."

As they sang, Coco remembered the necklace and took it from her pocket. Calling Ellie to her, she said, "We've got you a present"

"Have we?" said Dunc. "What present? I've already given her my biggest blackberries!"

"It's just a little trinket I found earlier. A necklace," she explained. Then Coco reached through the bars of the gate to hang it over Ellie's head.

In the sunlight, the pendant sparkled with many colours.

"Wow! Oh, thank you! It's lovely," remarked Ellie. "I can wear it at my party - if I have one!"

Then Onslow asked, "Where did you get *that* from?" While a curious Mort demanded to know how long she'd had it - and if it was actually hers to give away!

Coco held up her hand to stop the questioning. "Look," she answered, "I found it in the tree we were hiding in. A rabbit must have dug it up."

"That old tree... Bessie's Oak?" exclaimed Mort, pointing at it across the field.

Like Onslow, he vaguely recalled that Gascoyne had once told them to keep away from it, because it was 'special' for some reason!

"My dad calls that tree 'Elizabeth's Oak'," said Ellie.

But as she spoke, Onslow noticed something about the pendant. "Hey, look, it's the shape of the letter 'E' !" he said.

And, sure enough, when it was worn the the right way round it revealed an E.

"There you are!" said Coco. "It's even got your initial on it. E for Ellie."

This jogged Mort's memory again. "Yes, and E for Elizabeth too. And some girls called Elizabeth are also called Bess – as in 'Good Queen Bess'."

"Well, Elizabeth is my *real* name," said Ellie, "but they all call me Ellie instead. My mum says it's a nickname."

Dunc was a bit confused. "So, that tree has got two names?" he asked. "Bessie's Oak and Elizabeth's Oak?"

"Yes," said Mort, "but they both mean the same thing!"

Mortimerry told Ellie that Good Queen Bess was actually Queen Elizabeth the First, and she lived in Hatfield Palace when she was a girl.

"That's right," Flossie Jo continued. "And there is a famous story that one day, when she was a young princess in Hatfield, she was sitting under an oak tree when soldiers came to tell that her that she was going to be the Queen of England!"

Mortimerry gasped out loud. "That's Bessie's Oak! I remember now! It was the tree she used to read under. That's why Gascoyne said it was a special tree. Flossie Jo and Mort looked at each other in amazement. They realised what this might mean.

Ellie was amazed too. And pleased. "I've got the same name as a queen!" she said. "Great!"

Flossie Jo smiled at Ellie and said, "Apart from sharing her name, you may also have her necklace! Queen Elizabeth may have dropped it here hundreds of years ago!"

The Hobtails had a very close look at the necklace and they agreed that it looked like a valuable piece of jewellery.

"Oh good!" said Ellie. But she looked a little sad. "It's so special, you know, but if we sold it, I could have such a big party - and all my friends could come!"

Just then, Mr and Mrs Beech were heard talking as they made their way to the back garden.

Before the Hobtails disappeared, Flossie said, "Tell your mum and dad to take it to a museum. They'll know what to do, and maybe one day everybody will be able to see it."

Then she waved and hid with the others nearby, watching as Ellie ran back to her parents.

"Mummy! Daddy! I can have a big party now!" she said, excitedly showing them her necklace. "Look what Coco gave me! She called it a trinket, and we've got to take it to a museum."

Her parents studied the necklace and held it up to the sunlight where the coloured jewels glinted and gleamed. They came to realise that it was made of gold and diamonds.

"This is no mere *trinket*!" said Mrs Beech, in amazement. "This could be worth a fortune!"

Mr Beech smiled at his wife and held his daughter's hand. "Well, Ellie," he said, "you should be very grateful to your friend Coco - whoever she is - because if the museum want to buy it, we won't have to sell the cottage... or the woods."

Then Mr Beech lifted up his daughter and kissed her cheek. "Come on, birthday girl," he said, "let's see if the museum will let you have the best party ever!"

And, as the happy family walked to their car, an unmistakable figure flew across the sun, casting a large shadow which glided over the cottage roof.

It was Pellington, who had come to check on the young Hobtails.

"I'm sure I could hear explosions coming from this direction. Is everybody alright?" he asked.

"Yes. Fine, thanks," replied Mortimerry, shrugging his shoulders.

"We're just on our way home."

"Good. Gascoyne was beginning to worry," said Pellington. "So, what exactly *were* you doing over here?"

Flossie Jo winked at Dunc and laughed. "Oh, nothing much. Just saving private woods. That's all!"

THE END

The Hatfield

HOBTAILS

FLOSSIE JO

FROM OLD CHALK MINE TUNNELS
DEEP BENEATH THE STREETS OF
HATFIELD - COMES THE SOUND
OF THE UNDERGROUND .....
HOBMUSIC !

MORTIMERRY

WE'RE THE HOBTAILS

TALBOT

COCO

ONSLOW

www.hobtails.co.uk

£4.99